LISA LOEB'S
SILLY
SING-ALONG
THE DISAPPOINTING PANCAKE
AND OTHER ZANY SONGS

ILLUSTRATED BY RYAN O'ROURKE

STERLING CHILDREN'S BOOKS
New York

A big "Thank you, ma'am!" to my friends Alma Doll, who first showed me how
to finger pick on the guitar, and her sister Shannon, who reminded
me of some of those wonderful silly songs from our days at Camp Champions,
and to my sweet daughter, Lyla, who lights up when the singing starts.

STERLING CHILDREN'S BOOKS
New York

An Imprint of Sterling Publishing
387 Park Avenue South
New York, NY 10016

Text © 2011 by Lisa Loeb
Illustrations © 2011 by Ryan O'Rourke
Art direction and design by Merideth Harte

The artwork for this book was prepared using oils and acrylic on illustration board and wood, with some help from Photoshop and Illustrator.

ISBN 978-1-4027-6915-3 (Hardcover and CD)

Distributed in Canada by Sterling Publishing
c/o Canadian Manda Group, 165 Dufferin Street
Toronto, Ontario, Canada M6K 3H6
Distributed in the United Kingdom by GMC Distribution Services
Castle Place, 166 High Street, Lewes, East Sussex, England BN7 1XU
Distributed in Australia by Capricorn Link (Australia) Pty. Ltd.
P.O. Box 704, Windsor, NSW 2756, Australia

For information about custom editions, special sales, and premium and corporate purchases,
please contact Sterling Special Sales at 800-805-5489 or specialsales@sterlingpublishing.com.

Manufactured in China

Lot #:
2 4 6 8 10 9 7 5 3 1
07/11

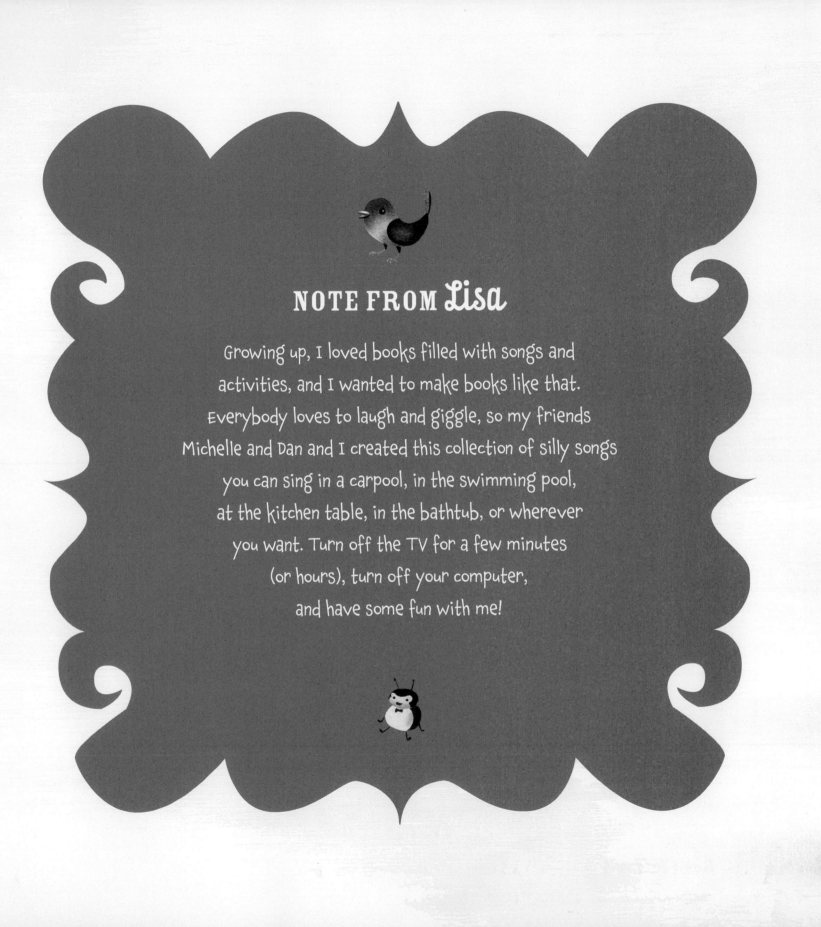

NOTE FROM Lisa

Growing up, I loved books filled with songs and
activities, and I wanted to make books like that.
Everybody loves to laugh and giggle, so my friends
Michelle and Dan and I created this collection of silly songs
you can sing in a carpool, in the swimming pool,
at the kitchen table, in the bathtub, or wherever
you want. Turn off the TV for a few minutes
(or hours), turn off your computer,
and have some fun with me!

Opposite Day

I woke up this morning and the moon was still high.
There was snow on the front yard in the month of July.
I put on my pajamas when I jumped out of bed,
then I fell to the ceiling and I stood on my head.

I ran to the kitchen and I asked my mom,
"What in the bananas is going on?"
She served spaghetti for my breakfast
with a side of flan, and she said,

Everything is opposite on Opposite Day.
Things just happen in the opposite way.
When your flippity flop is kinda floppity flay,
it must be Opposite Day.

There were squirrels in the water and fish in the trees.
Cars were going backwards down the opposite streets.
You gotta finish your cake before your carrots and peas,
put your napkin on your head, and don't say please.

Everything is opposite on Opposite Day.
Everything goes in the opposite way.
The cats all bark and the dogs meow.
Left is right and up is down.

Everything is opposite on Opposite Day.
Things just happen in the opposite way.
When your flippity flop is kinda floppity flay,
it must be Opposite Day.

You don't have to worry if something is wrong.
It's just a different view of the same.
It all may seem so strange, but tomorrow it may change.
So just enjoy today—it's Opposite Day.

Everything is opposite on Opposite Day.
Things just happen in the opposite way.
When your flippity flop is kinda floppity flay,
it must be Opposite Day.

Make up a story about your own OPPOSITE DAY. What are your SILLIEST, most **topsy-turvy** answers to these questions?

What time does your day start?

What clothes do you put on?

WHAT MOOD ARE YOU IN?

What do you see out the window?

What do you eat for breakfast?

What do you learn at school?

HOW DOES YOUR DAY END?

I'M A Little COCONUT

I'M A LITTLE COCONUT is a fun, silly song I used to sing at summer camp when I was a kid. This song, like many others, can be sung with or without an instrument accompanying you. You can clap along and when you get to the end, you can start over and sing it even faster.

I'm a little coconut sitting in my coco hut.
Someone came and sat on me.
That is why I'm cracked, you see.
I'm a nut, CLAP-CLAP (two fast CLAPS)
in a rut, CLAP-CLAP. (two fast CLAPS)
I'm a nut in a rut, I am, CLAP-CLAP. (two fast CLAPS)

I'm a little junior miss. I can hug and I can kiss.
I can sing and I can dance.
I wear ruffles on my...
Whoops! boys, take another guess.
I wear ruffles on my dress.
I'm a nut, CLAP-CLAP (two fast CLAPS)
in a rut, CLAP-CLAP. (two fast CLAPS)
I'm a nut in a rut, I am, CLAP-CLAP. (two fast CLAPS)

WHOOPS!
{throw your hands up & say this very high}

I'm a little piece of tin.
Nobody knows what shape I'm in.
Got four wheels and a running board.
I'm a four-door, I'm a Ford.

Honk honk rattle rattle rattle crash beep beep!
Honk honk rattle rattle rattle crash beep beep!
Honk honk rattle rattle rattle crash beep beep!

{ USE THESE MOTIONS }

HONK
{pull one ear}

HONK
{pull other ear}

RATTLE
{shake...}

RATTLE
{your . . .}

RATTLE
{head!}

CRASH
{tap chin with your palm}

BEEP! BEEP!
{tap your nose twice)

Honk honk honk beep beep. Ahoooga!

AHOOOGA!

{pretend you are honking a truck horn!}

COCONUT CREAM "PIE"
This song reminds me of a
tasty treat that I eat
as a snack, as a dessert,
and sometimes even
for breakfast!

IN A BOWL, LAYER:
A big dollop of plain, unsweetened **yogurt**

THEN...
Half a pre-chilled **banana**, sliced

THEN...
A tablespoon of shredded, toasted **coconut**

THEN...
Slide one panel of a
graham cracker against the side
of the bowl.

The DISAPPOINTING PANCAKE

It's always breakfast Thursday nights for dinnertime.
Orange juice, oatmeal, eggs, and waffles served at five.
But once there was something I didn't recognize.
It was harder than the table, so I thought it was my plate.
I hit it with a hammer, but it wouldn't even break.
It slipped upon some syrup and the butter ricocheted.
Then it rolled and it rolled and it rolled
and it rolled, the disappointing pancake.

Rolling toward the baseball field just down the road.
The pitcher on the mound was winding up to throw.
The crowd yelled, "Batter, batter!" He felt so at home.
He rolled right up to the catcher, who had somehow lost his mitt,
who put the pancake on his hand and like a glove it fit.
And then he caught the final ball he surely would have missed.
And they cheered and they cheered and they cheered
and they cheered for the disappointing pancake.

The catcher tossed his pancake mitt into the sky.
The wind picked up, the pancake soared four miles high.
And when it finally landed, it was just in time
for a bike rider who hit a bump, his tire needed air.
The pancake rolled right in and made a temporary spare.
He pedaled to the bike shop where they'd get a quick repair.
And they rode and they rode and they rode
and they rode on the disappointing pancake.

It was a manhole cover in Manhattan,
a lily pad in Padua,
a sombrero in some little town in Spain.
A satellite in Saddle River,
a knee patch in Saskatchewan,
a coaster on the chilly coast of Maine.
The pancake made its way around the world,
jumping in and helping where he could.
Then I looked outside and saw a glow.
Maybe it's the moon or just a UFO?

The pancake fell down from the heavens to my bed,
and landed like a pillow underneath my head,
where I dreamt sweet pancake dreams as I slept.
The pancake disappointed me at breakfast, yes, it's true.
But there are many other things that this pancake can do.
I'd like to think that pancakes are a bit like me and you.
And we roll and we roll and we roll and we roll
like a disappointing pancake.
We roll and we roll and we roll and we roll
like a disappointing pancake.
We roll and we roll and we roll and we roll,
not so disappointing pancake.

Fried Ham

FRIED HAM is definitely a hot summer silly song! My niece and I were most recently singing it in the pool on our family vacation. We spent the day swimming and eating grilled cheese sandwiches, French fries, lollipops, ice cream, and carrot sticks, so it was especially fun to sing this silly list of snacks.

This song is only as long as your imagination . . . or as long as no one stops you!

Fried ham, fried ham, cheese and baloney.
And after the macaroni
we'll have onions, pickles, and pretzels, and
then we'll have some more fried ham, fried ham.

Now repeat each new verse in a different voice.

You can sing it in any style or accent you can imagine. "Worse" is really just another word for sillier!

Next verse, same as the first.

TEXAS ACCENT

makes it worse.

{ WITH A TWANG! }

Next verse, same as the first.

OPERA VOICE

makes it worse.

{ HOW HIGH CAN YOU SING? }

Next verse, same as the first.

UNDERWATER

makes it worse.

{ BRUSH YOUR LIPS WITH YOUR FINGER }

French Accent

baby voice

ENGLISH ACCENT

EVERYBODY DREAMS

I was over at Dan and Michelle's house recording some new songs, and their dog Bea was twitching in her sleep. We wondered, "What is she dreaming about? Chasing squirrels? Talking to a cat? Digging for a bone in the backyard?" This inspired us to write a song about animals' dreams and even our own dreams. What do you dream about? What does your pet dream about?

Does a bear dream of honey?
Does the honey dream of bees?
Do dogs dream of bunnies?
Does a cracker dream of cheese?

Does an otter dream of water?
Does a penguin dream of ice?
Does a Beatle dream of
holding hands?
A weevil dream of rice?

Dreams, everybody dreams.
Everybody dreams.
Close your eyes and dream.

Do butterflies dream of popcorn?
Does a porcupine dream of hugs?
Does a puffin dream of muffins?
Does a question dream of shrugs?

Does an ocelot dream a little?
Does a shrimp dream a lot?
Does a moose dream of chocolate?
Does a leopard dream of spots?

Dreams, everybody dreams.
Everybody dreams.
Close your eyes and dream.

Does a firefly dream of
midnight skies?
A lizard dream of leaps?
Does a clownfish dream he's funny?
Does a parrot's dream repeat?

Do pandas dream in colors
and peacocks in black and white?
If a jellyfish dreams of
peanut butter,
do starfish dream of night?

Last night I had this crazy dream.
I was wondering what it means.
There was a spaceman,
he was looking at me
out of his rocket ship
into the tiny window
of my superstar golden van.

Everybody dreams.
Everybody dreams.
Close your eyes and dream.

Does a mole dream a horizon?
Does an eagle dream of land?
Does a lichen dream of
swimming free?
A puppet dream of hands?

Does a monkey dream of uncles?
Does an aardvark dream of ants?
Does a snail dream of running fast?
A baboon dream of pants?

Dreams, everybody dreams.
Everybody dreams.
Close your eyes and dream.

CHEWING GUM

My mother gave me a quarter to tip the porter.
I did not tip the porter. I bought some chewing gum.

Chew-la-la-la-la chewing gum, chew-la-la chewing gum.
Chew-la-la-la-la chewing gum, chew-la-la chewing gum.

My mother gave me a dime to buy a lime.
I did not buy a lime. I bought some chewing gum.

Chew-la-la-la-la chewing gum, chew-la-la chewing gum.
Chew-la-la-la-la chewing gum, chew-la-la chewing gum.

My mother gave me a nickel to buy a pickle.
I did not buy a pickle. I bought some chewing gum.

Chew-la-la-la-la chewing gum, chew-la-la chewing gum.
Chew-la-la-la-la chewing gum, chew-la-la chewing gum.

My mother gave me a penny to buy some chewing gum.
I did not buy some chewing gum.
I'm sick of chewing gum!

When we used to sing this song at summer camp, this is the hand motion that went with it.

{ PART 1 }

Twirl wad of "gum" out of your mouth

  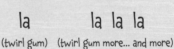 

Chew	la	la la la	chewing gum,*
	(twirl gum)	(twirl gum more... and more)	(and the most!)

{ PART 2 }

Twirl "gum" back into your mouth

chew   la la   chewing gum.

AND REPEAT!

* NOTE: This is make-believe, pretend, not real chewing gum.

A CO DI BY DOZE
(A COLD IN MY NOSE)

I called up my friend the other day
to see if he could come over and play.
He picked up his phone and his voice sounded strange,
and I couldn't make out a word he was saying.

A co di by doze, a co di by doze,
I got a co di by doze.
A co di by doze, a co di by doze,
I got a co di by doze.

Baby by baba will bake doodle soup.
Baby by baba will bake doodle soup?
Baby by baba will bake doodle soup!
Oh, your mama will make noodle soup!
By baba will bake doodle soup!

A co di by doze, a co di by doze,
I got a co di by doze.
A co di by doze, a co di by doze,
I got a co di by doze.

I dee da go dake a dap in by bed.
I dee da go dake a dap in by bed?
I dee da go dake a dap in by bed!
Oh, you need to go nap in your bed!
I dee da go dap in by bed.

A co di by doze, a co di by doze,
I got a co di by doze.
A co di by doze, a co di by doze,
I got a co di by doze.

I dee da spood da bedicid.
I dee da spood da bedicid?
I dee da spood da bedicid!
Oh, you need a spoon of medicine!
I dee da spood da bedicid!

A co di by doze, a co di by doze,
I got a co di by doze.
A co di by doze, a co di by doze,
I got a co di by doze.

YUMM!

This song was written with the joy of mis-hearing in mind. When you have a really bad cold with a stuffy nose, or "doze," as this flu-ish character sings, sometimes other people can't understand what you're saying. This is either very frustrating or hilarious, depending on how you look at it, which brings me to one of my favorite games . . .

THE TELEPHONE GAME
This game is best played with as many people as possible . . .

1. Sit in a circle on the floor, or around a table (especially at a loud restaurant while you're celebrating someone's birthday).

2. The game starts when someone whispers a short phrase into the ear of the person sitting next to them. Careful not to let anyone else hear!

3. Then the phrase is repeated into the next person's ear and is passed along from person to person until it reaches the person who started. That person then announces the phrase for everyone to hear. You'll be surprised to hear how it's changed into something different than how it started!

The BANJO SONG

This is an incredible little ditty. The words tell the story of a broken banjo, and at the same time they sound like a banjo being played.

Whenever I sing this song in concert, Daru, who sings harmony with me and also plays many different instruments, always laughs. Also, I made a real, professional banjo player laugh when I sang this song for him. Another silly song I learned at camp!

I u-lu-lu-lused to play-lay-lay
my o-lo-lold ban-jo-lo-lo
and re-le-lest it o-lo-lon
my knee-lee-lee-lee-lee-lee-lee.
But now-low-low the stri-li-li-lings
are bro-lo-lo-ken u-lu-lup,
and i-li-lit's no goo-loo-lood
to me-lee-lee-lee-lee-lee-lee.

I to-loo-look it to-loo-loo
the me-le-lender's sho-lo-lop
to see-lee-lee what he-lee-lee
could do-loo-loo-loo-loo-loo-loo.
And now-low-low the stri-li-lings
are fi-li-lixed u-lu-lup,
and i-li-lit's as goo-loo-lood
as new-loo-loo-loo-loo-loo-loo.

SIPPIN' CIDER

The cutest boy I ever saw
was sippin' cider through a straw.
The cutest boy I ever saw
was sippin' cidi-idi-ider through a straw.

First cheek to cheek, then jaw to jaw,
we sipped our cider through a straw.
First cheek to cheek then jaw to jaw
we sipped our cidi-idi-ider through a straw.

The straw did slip, then lip to lip,
we sipped our cider through a straw.
The straw did slip then lip to lip
we sipped our cidi-idi-ider through a straw.

That's how I got my mother-in-law
and 49 kids who call me Ma.
That's how I got my mother-in-law
and 49 kids who call me Ma.

The moral of this story is
don't sip your cider through a straw.
The moral of this story is
don't sip your cidi-idi-ider through a straw.
Drink ginger ale!

CATERPILLAR TRICK

1. Carefully tear off the end of the straw wrapper.

2. Inch the wrapper off little by little, trying not to tear it. Instead, scrunch it up like a tiny, squished accordion. (It might tear a little.)

3. Gently slide the scrunched paper off the straw and put it on the table.

4. Get a small bit of liquid in your straw by dipping your straw in your glass and then putting your thumb over the end of the straw.

5. Then let a few drops of liquid drip onto the scrunched up straw wrapper and your "caterpillar" will come alive!!

FOUND A PEANUT

This song takes us on the haphazard journey of a person who eats a peanut that's so rotten it kills them. (But don't worry. You'll find out why.) Lots of adventures happen along the way, and then, yet another peanut is found and everything starts over again!

If you're not allergic to peanuts, you just can't help yourself sometimes. I love peanuts even more than I love long songs.

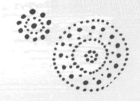

Found a peanut, found a peanut,
found a peanut just now.
Just now I found a peanut.
Found a peanut just now.

Cracked it open, cracked it open,
cracked it open just now.
Just now I cracked it open.
Cracked it open just now.

It was rotten, it was rotten,
it was rotten just now.
Just now it was rotten.
It was rotten just now.

Ate it anyway, ate it anyway,
ate it anyway just now.
Just now I ate it anyway.
Ate it anyway just now.

Got a stomachache, got a stomachache,
got a stomachache just now.
Just now I got a stomachache.
Got a stomachache just now.

Called the doctor, called the doctor,
called the doctor just now.
Just now I called the doctor.
Called the doctor just now.

Operation, operation,
operation just now.
Just now an operation.
An operation just now.

Died anyway, died anyway,
died anyway just now.
Just now I died anyway.
Died anyway just now.

Went to heaven, went to heaven,
went to heaven just now.
Just now I went to heaven.
Went to heaven just now.

Wouldn't take me, wouldn't take me,
wouldn't take me just now.
Just now heaven wouldn't take me.
Wouldn't take me just now.

Went the other way,
went the other way,
went the other way just now.
Just now I went the other way.
Went the other way just now.

Was a dream, was a dream,
was a dream just now.
Just now it was a dream.
Was a dream just now.

Then I woke up, then I woke up,
then I woke up just now.
Just now I woke up.
I woke up just now.

And found a peanut,
found a peanut,
found a peanut just now.
Just now I found a peanut.
Found a peanut just now.

Here we go again!

CREDITS

OPPOSITE DAY
Written by Lisa Loeb, Dan Petty, and
  Michelle Lewis
Furious Rose Music (BMI), Bambalam
  Music (BMI), Bea the Dog Music
  (ASCAP)
Vocals: Lisa Loeb
Guitar, keyboards: Dan Petty
Bass: Curt Schneider
Drums: Blair Sinta
Background vocals: Michelle Lewis
Additional background vocals:
  Afternoon Campers

I'M A LITTLE COCONUT
Vocals: Lisa Loeb
Guitar: Dan Petty
Background vocals: Michelle Lewis

THE DISAPPOINTING PANCAKE
Written by Lisa Loeb, Dan Petty, and
  Michelle Lewis
Furious Rose Music (BMI), Bambalam
  Music (BMI), Bea the Dog Music
  (ASCAP)
Vocals, acoustic guitar: Lisa Loeb
Guitar, mandolin: Dan Petty
Banjo: Steve Martin
Bass: Leland Sklar
Drums: Jay Bellerose
Piano: Doug Petty

FRIED HAM
Vocals: Lisa Loeb
Guitar: Dan Petty
Background vocals: Afternoon Campers

EVERYBODY DREAMS
Written by Lisa Loeb, Dan Petty, and
  Michelle Lewis
Furious Rose Music (BMI), Bambalam
  Music (BMI), Bea the Dog Music
  (ASCAP)
Vocals, acoustic guitar: Lisa Loeb
Bass: Curt Schneider
Drums: Blair Sinta
Electric guitar and percussion: Dan Petty
Background vocals: Michelle Lewis

CHEWING GUM
Vocals, guitar: Lisa Loeb
Background vocals: Afternoon Campers

A CO DI BY DOZE
(A Cold in My Nose)
Written by Lisa Loeb, Dan Petty, and
  Michelle Lewis
Furious Rose Music (BMI), Bambalam
  Music (BMI), Bea the Dog Music
  (ASCAP)
Vocals, guitar: Lisa Loeb
Guitar: Dan Petty
Vocals: Isabel Petty

THE BANJO SONG
Vocals, guitar: Lisa Loeb
Mandolin: Dan Petty

SIPPIN' CIDER
Vocals, guitar: Lisa Loeb
Background vocals: Afternoon Campers

FOUND A PEANUT
Vocals: Lisa Loeb
Guitar, ukulele: Dan Petty

Afternoon Campers:
  Isabel Petty, Olive Petty,
  Zoe Eisenstein, Henry Eisenstein,
  Georgica Pettus, Harry Pettus

Produced by Lisa Loeb, Dan Petty, and
  Michelle Lewis
Recorded and Engineered by Dan Petty
  at The Path, Valley Village, CA

All songs mixed by Dan Petty at The Path
  except "The Disappointing Pancake"
  mixed by Bob Clearmountain, Mix This!
Mix This! Assistant: Brandon Duncan

Mastered by Hans DeKline

Special thanks to Frances Gilbert,
  Robert Agis, Merideth Harte,
  Judi Powers, and everyone at Sterling

Management: Janet Billig Rich,
  Manage This!
Legal Representation: Adam Ritholz,
  Ritholz, Levy, Sanders, Chidikel &
  Fields LLP
Business Management: Carrie Malcolm
  with Yana Konstantinovskaya, CRM
  Management LLC

For more information please go to
www.lisaloeb.com

For more information on the Camp Lisa
Foundation, go to www.camplisa.com

The Camp Lisa Foundation proudly
supports Summer Camp Opportunities
Provide an Edge, Inc. (SCOPE), a
nonprofit organization providing
children in need the edge to succeed
in life through the summer camp
experience. www.scope-ny.org

CONTACT: Lisa Loeb, 11054 Ventura Blvd. #381,
Studio City, CA 91604